Sonnie's library

My African Grandma

by

Sonnie L. Isemede & Karin Ezeakor

...d by **Prosenjit Roy**

To Papi and Grandma

My name is Sonnie Londynn. I am seven years old. I live in a very big house with my Mom, Dad and my little brother Nicholas who I call Nick. Also, in my house are my Grandma, Grandpa, Uncle Enahoro, my Aunty Nicole who I call Aunty Ko and my pet hermit crab who sleeps all day and is awake at night.

We are originally from Nigeria, West Africa. I have never been to Nigeria, but Grandma promised to take me there someday. Grandma teaches me about Nigeria culture by making Nigerian foods for me. My favorite Nigerian food is 'eba and okra soup'. Grandma says that Nigerian foods are always healthy and fresh because it comes straight from the farm to the market. Grandma remembers this because her mom, my great Grandma used to have a farm in Nigeria.

Grandma said there are many languages in Nigeria. Mom said Grandma started speaking our native language, Affemai with me when I was three years old. Grandma encourages me to speak Affemai even though I can't speak it well. Grandma says things to me in Affemai. I usually respond in English. She likes that I can understand what she says. She calls on me to speak Affemai when her friends are around. Grandma gets very happy when I try.

I enjoy watching Nigerian movies with my Grandma. She explains the movies to me when I don't understand them. This makes me happy because it helps me understand Nigerian culture better. Grandma calls Nigerian movies, Nollywood movies.

Grandma says there are lots of religions in Nigeria. There are Christians, Muslims and traditionalists. We are Christians and so we go to church. Grandma loves going to church. She always takes my brother and I to church with her.

We go early to help clean the church. Whenever we get to church, she says, "Sonnie, it's important that we help clean and set the church up because it is the house of God." Grandma gives me a washcloth to help her clean the chairs for church members. I feel special because Grandma trusts me with important chores. After church, people come up to my Grandma to thank her for getting the Church all cleaned up. Grandma tells them that I helped, and the church members thank me too.

I enjoy going to the tailor's with Grandma. When I was three years, she took me to a Nigerian tailor to make me a Nigerian dress. Since then, whenever my Grandma goes to the tailor, she lets me tag along. Grandma takes forever at the tailor's discussing styles, fabric and when she needs it to be ready. Sometimes, I get bored and play with fabric pieces on the floor.

I love to draw, and my favourite thing to draw are fashion styles. One day, my Grandma saw my drawing book and the styles I have been thinking about. "Sonnie, can I have a look?" Grandma said excitedly. My Grandma became obsessed with my drawing since she saw my book. She was so excited, she started to teach me how to sew. She bought me my own little sewing machine and now, we sew together.

Grandma rarely goes out, but when she does, she buys me things for sewing. Right now, I sew for my barbie's and teddy bear's. My grandma bought me confetti to decorate my doll's clothes. Sometimes, after school, my Grandma watches me draw and sew. She always makes sure that I use up any cloth I begin sewing with. These are my favorite moments with my Grandma.

My Grandma loves to cook and asks me to join her in the kitchen especially when she makes Nigerian food. She always makes me sit on the kitchen counter to watch. She gives me chores to do like grabbing the spices from the cupboard. Grandma's cooking looks hard, but she says "Sonnie, you have to start small."

I love baking with my Grandma. Every weekend, my Grandma makes sure we bake something. She lets my brother and I lick the batter. My brother also likes when Grandma lets him help. He likes to mix the batter, but he ends up getting the kitchen counter messy. Grandma always scolds him softly saying "Nicholas you are too impatient." Whenever I like a food that Grandma doesn't know how to make, we watch a video and learn how to make it together. Grandma doesn't like it when I give up on something because I don't know how to do it. She will always say, "Sonnie, you have to try."

Grandma loves to tell my brother and I traditional Nigerian tales. She told us about how the tortoise tricked the elephant, which is my favorite tale. Sometimes, Grandma reads to us. Whenever she reads Aladdin, she pronounces it "Allah dean." It makes me giggle a lot and I say to her "Grandma it is not Allah dean, it's Aladdin."

Every night, after Grandma tells us stories about her childhood or tales from Nigeria, my Grandma tells us to kneel beside her by the bed and bow our heads while she prays for us. Sometimes, she will read a verse from the Bible, and she will ask us what we understand from it. She always explains what it means, what God wants us to do and how God wants us to live. She always reminds me to pray.

Grandma makes my brother and I sing songs in Affemai. I don't get all the words right, but my Grandma smiles and sings along with me in a soft beautiful voice. After prayers, my Grandma gives us a big hug before saying goodnight.

My Grandma speaks differently when she talks, mom calls it an accent. She pronounces things differently than I do. She always says "I am proud of my accent. It gives me character and lets the world know where I am from." Sometimes, she pronounces things in a way that makes me giggle. When I say, "Grandma that's not how to say that" she always smiles back and says "Sonnie, I love my accent".

When Grandma is not around, I try to imitate her accent. I try to sound like her especially when I'm talking to my Dad or Mom or my little brother. My brother loves when I speak like Grandma. It was hard to understand Grandma at first, but listening has helped. When Grandma and my Dad talk in Affemai, I listen a lot because I want to learn how to speak just like Grandma. When I'm alone, I try to pronounce new words or say sentences out loud. One day, I believe I will speak to Grandma in Affemai.

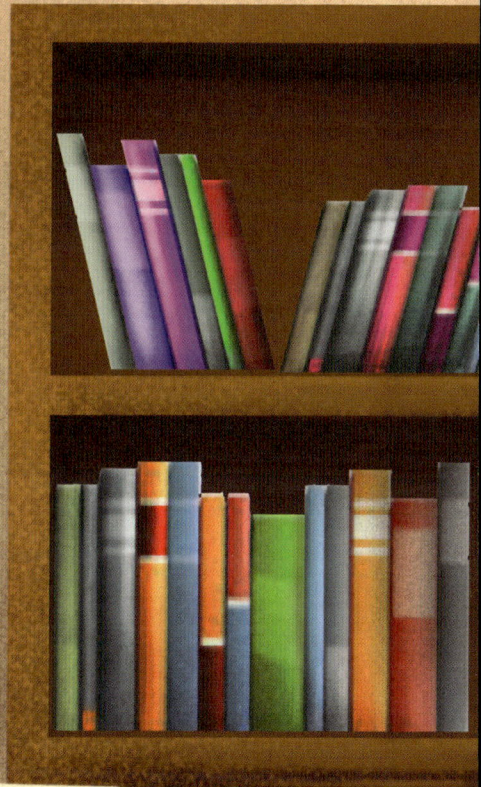

I love my Grandma a lot. She comforts me when I cry. When I get into trouble with my parents, she lets me hide in her room. I share a lot of hobbies with my Grandma, and I'm happiest when I'm spending time with her. My Grandma is patient, strong and kind. She teaches me a lot of things and lets me know that anything I want to do is possible. Whenever we pray before I go to sleep, I always ask God to protect my family, especially my Grandma. I go to sleep smiling knowing that tomorrow I get to spend another day with her.

Seven things Grandma told me about Africa

1. Africa is the second largest continent in the world.

2. There are 54 countries in Africa.

3. The longest river in the world is the River Nile, and it's in Africa.

4. The richest person ever is African, his name is Mansa Musa.

5. The African elephant is the world's largest land animal, they are gigantic.

6. Africa has the largest population of black people.

7. African has the best natural resources like gold, silver, and crude oil for making gas for cars.

Printed in Great Britain
by Amazon